PERSEPHONE AUTUMN

BETWEEN WORDS PUBLISHING LLC

ISBN: 978-1-951477-40-0 (Ebook)

ISBN: 978-1-951477-41-7 (Paperback)

Editor: Ellie McLove | My Brother's Editor

Cover Design: Persephone Autumn | Between Words Publishing LLC

sweetest
DEVOTION
devotion series
PERSEPHONE
AUTUMN

Devotion Series

Distorted Devotion

Undying Devotion

Beloved Devotion

Darkest Devotion

Sweetest Devotion

Bay Area Duet Series

Click Duet

Through the Lens

Time Exposure

Inked Duet

Fine Line

Love Buzz

Insomniac Duet

Restless Night

A Love So Bright

Artist Duet

Blank Canvas

Abstract Passion

<u>Novellas</u>

Reese

Penny

<u>Lake Lavender Series</u>

Depths Awakened

One Night Forsaken

Every Thought Taken

<u>Stone Bay Series</u>

Broken Sky — Prequel

<u>Standalone Romance Novels</u>

Sweet Tooth

Transcendental

<u>Poetry Collections</u>

Ink Veins

Broken Metronome

Slipping From Existence

PUBLISHED UNDER P. AUTUMN

<u>Standalone Non-Romance Novels</u>

By Dawn

To those that have seen the darkest side of life, but didn't let it pull you all the way under. To those that found a reason to keep going each day.

ONE

JENSEN

Fifteen hours on the road over two days was worth every muscle spasm, horn honk, and dispute over where to stop for decent food or a clean restroom. Because finally, we reached our destination.

Mom parks in the driveway of the cedar-shingled cottage we will call home for the next seven days. A vacation to celebrate my twenty-second birthday tomorrow. I told her a trip wasn't necessary—twenty-two isn't one of the major milestone birthdays, not like eighteen or twenty-one—but she refused to listen. Neither would Ma. In fact, both were adamant about celebrating me as much as humanly possible. I indulged them.

Dr. Tiffany Page and Eliza Warren. The best two mothers a guy could ask for. Two of the most incredible women. They spoil me—more with love, but also with gifts—because of my rocky past. Although unnecessary, they feel it is their duty to make up for all the atrocious things my birth parents did during my adolescence.

Just having them in my life, though, is all I will ever need. Their constant love and support and positivity is the beacon I never knew I always needed. What would always bring me back to the light.

And Samantha. Sam. The most extraordinary girlfriend. A woman I am damn lucky to call mine. A remarkable woman that healed my heart while I healed hers.

I peek over at her as she unbuckles her belt and shoulders her purse. Her messy dark locks mask her profile, but I easily picture the excited smile on her lips. The gleam in her eyes. I live for that smile, that shine.

She opens the car door and slides out of the SUV. When I don't join her after a beat, she peers back into the car, brows pinched together. "You planning to stay in the car?" she teases.

Unbuckling my belt, I exit the car and sidle up to her. Inhale her sweet magnolia scent and close my eyes briefly. Get lost in her presence and warmth.

Will I ever get my fill of her? Nope, absolutely not.

"Nah. Was caught up in you is all."

Her hand slaps my bicep playfully as she rolls her eyes. "Always trying to sweet-talk me."

"Is it working?"

Twisting into my frame, she hugs my side and kisses my cheek. Warmth spreads from where her lips touched my skin to the center of my chest. "Always."

Ma walks back to the car from the cottage. Excitement lights her expression while the idea of time away relaxes her frame. Much as she loves her job, she doesn't grant herself time off often enough. Neither does Mom. Which is why I would never deny them family trips, no matter how old I am.

"You two gonna stand there gawking outside all day?"

"No, Miss Liz," Sam says as she follows her to the back of the car.

Ma comes to an abrupt halt, spins to face Sam and the two almost collide. Bringing hands to her biceps, Ma holds her at arm's length. "I know you mean well, but please, for the love of God, call me Liz or Ma. We're not strangers. You can drop the Miss business. Makes me sound old or snooty."

Sam winces and it is adorable as hell. "Sorry, Miss…" She clamps down on her lips, takes a deep breath, then starts again. "Sorry, Ma. Old habits."

With a gentle smile and a pat on the arm, Ma says, "I know. They're not bad habits. But you're family. No need for formalities."

Sam is family because she matters—to me, and to our unconventional family. Fingers crossed, one day I hope to call her family for an entirely different reason.

We lug the suitcases from the car and wheel them inside the cottage. From the outside, the place appears small and quaint. The perfect place for a getaway. Enough room to sleep and dine and not much else.

Stepping inside, I'm reminded to never judge something or someone by outward appearance. Because the cottage exterior is an illusion compared to the grandeur within the walls.

The cottage is spacious and bright and open. Floor-to-ceiling windows inhabit each room and gift us a view of the evergreen-lined beach. Invisible from the street view is a lower level with bedrooms facing the coast. A wraparound wood deck with Adirondack chairs allows for the perfect view of the sunset. Which I plan to watch with my girl every night.

Down a short hallway, I steer us into the smaller room on the right. Deposit our bags on the bed Sam and I will share while here. Step to the window and take in the scenery. Breathe deep and try to settle my nerves.

This vacation was planned to celebrate my birthday, an occasion I never enjoyed until my moms came into my life. But that isn't what has me on edge. I have other plans mapped out this week. Plans that scare me to death.

Warm hands wrap around my waist, followed by a kiss on my upper back. I blanket her embrace with my arms and hold Sam impossibly closer to my frame. Bask in her warmth and touch.

God, I love her.

"It's beautiful here," she whispers as she rests her cheek on my spine.

"It is." I lift her hand to my lips and kiss her knuckles. "Let's unpack then go exploring."

She nods and reluctantly releases me from her hold.

We unpack our suitcases, stash our clothes in the closet and dresser, and toiletries in the en suite bathroom. With our belongings in their temporary home, we wander back to the open living room and kitchen at the heart of the cottage. As expected, Ma is in the kitchen unloading the cooler and organizing the space. Mom has already cozied up on the chair near the window with a book.

"Is it cool if we take the car and go explore downtown?" I ask Ma as I snag a banana from the counter.

Scooping the keys off the counter, she hands them over. "Only if you'll do me a favor before you return."

"Of course."

She hands me a slip of paper and cash. "Stop at the market for a few things."

My eyes drop down to the list and note that *a few things* equal twenty-plus items. Not that I expect less. I can't argue, though. Nor would I want to. I owe these two incredible women everything and more. They rescued me from hell.

"Sure thing."

Mom marks the page of her book and joins the conversation. "Oh, and let us know what shops and restaurants you find. Or if you want to have your birthday dinner at one of them."

"Will do."

Sam and I start for the door, get within two feet of our getaway, and Ma chimes in again. "Ooh. See if they have a farmers' market too." A dreamy look steals her expression. "I love farmers' markets."

I reach for the door handle and twist. "I'll keep ya posted," I say as I all but shove Sam out the door. "We'll be back."

Soon as we hit the deck and the door closes behind us, I sigh and Sam chuckles. I love my moms more than anything, but sometimes they make me delirious. I hope to not be as needy—or excited about groceries and produce—in my midthirties. Then again, life could be much worse.

Unlocking the car, I open the passenger door for Sam then dash around to the driver's side, hop in and crank the engine.

I twist to face her after adjusting the mirrors. "Ready to explore?"

My favorite smile dons her face as she takes my hand. "I'm ready for everything."

Me too, sweetheart. Me too.

His hand in mine, Jensen guides us through downtown Cannon Beach. From some online search history, I knew this was a small town. What I didn't know was how cute and quaint it was here.

We coast down the street and take in the small town so completely opposite of the big city life we live in Southern California. I have always loved city life and sunny beaches. Boutiques and restaurants and endless things to do, all easily accessible in the city. But as I stare out the window and eye the passing storefronts, this charming town has my heart fluttering.

Jensen parallel parks on the street and cuts the engine. "Ready?" he asks after a squeeze of my hand.

I unbuckle my seat belt and bounce a little in my seat. "Yes."

Over the next two hours, Jensen and I wander the main drag of downtown. We enter countless shops filled with homemade soaps, handmade jewelry, and everything from clothes to furniture. In each store, I search for the perfect keepsake to buy to remember this trip. As of yet, nothing sparks my eye.

Jensen points to an ice cream and candy shop. "That has your name written all over it."

I hug his side and push up on my toes to kiss his cheek. "You know me too well."

He twists to kiss my lips. "Not possible. I learn something new about you every day."

Steering us into the shop, I spin and walk backward, facing Jensen. "Oh yeah?"

He nods.

"And what did you learn about me today?" Challenge with a hint of amusement layers my tone.

The right corner of his mouth kicks up. "That my favorite piece of sunshine in your blue eyes sparkles more in this small town than it ever has in the city."

Growing up, most kids my age picked on me because my eyes were "funny looking." Navy-blue rim, cloudy sky-blue center, and a small orange spot near the outer base of my pupil. I'd heard all the cruel opinions —mostly from girls. My eyes were defective. It was a poop spot. Those were from the younger years. As I entered high school, it turned uglier. That my mother had an affair or I was adopted and didn't know it.

As strong as I tried to be, as much as I tried to ignore their hurtful words, they still stung.

Until Jensen.

The moment Jensen entered my life, everything changed. He gave me a new outlook. Lifted me up when others had shoved me down for so long. Jensen has this uncanny ability to make me smile, even on the worst days. He adds this extra blip to my pulse and stutter to my breath.

Granted, we hadn't met under the best circumstances. No one dreams of finding love in a psychiatric facility. Our individual histories may be vastly different, but our hearts were so heavy during that time. Seeing Jensen each day during that dark period… it gifted me with new perspective. Made me feel all the love I had missed for so many years.

Jensen and I didn't fall in love at Lewis House. We fell in like. Bonded over situations other people may not fully comprehend. Became the best of friends after we left. And slowly, that friendship turned into the most incredible and unbreakable love.

I love that our past isn't pretty or perfect. That we aren't some picturesque relationship model. Our love has cuts and bruises and scars. It also has tenderness and devotion and promise rings.

My thumb traces the thin gold band with a small opal and diamond chips on either side. Jensen's promise to always be mine. Not like I needed a ring for such a vow, but it makes me love him even more.

"And I've never seen your eyes twinkle this much since we pulled up to the cottage." I stick out my tongue and haul him into me for a kiss.

Two older women a few feet away snicker before one of them says, "How I miss young love."

As we break free, the smell of the shop finally hits my nose. Chocolate and cinnamon. Vanilla and caramel. Freshly baked waffle cones and sweet cream. Pure heaven.

Inhaling deeply, I hug Jensen's side and squeeze his bicep. "I want one of everything." Of course, this is an exaggeration. There have to be a thousand different types of sweets in the store. Homemade candy, fudge, and ice cream options galore. Stumbling across old sweet shops like this is rare, but they are gold mines.

But that doesn't stop Jensen. And his next words don't surprise in the least. "Better start filling a bag now. Might be here until close."

I squeal, kiss his cheek and skip over to the bag holder like a seven-year-old. Jensen simply laughs in my wake and helps me pluck candy from bins. I fill the bag to the brim in no time. We wander to the cases with homemade candies and fudge, studying them all before making selections for us and the moms. Then, no surprise, I order a waffle cone loaded with marionberry pie ice cream.

Jensen pays for my sugar habit and we exit the shop. Parking on the bench outside, we share the cone and people watch.

"You know," I say as I hold the cone for Jensen to lick. "Never really thought I'd be a small-town girl." My eyes shift up the street and survey the cedar-shingled stores and cheery-eyed pedestrians. "But I like this place. More than expected." I return my gaze to Jensen, a knowing smile on his lips. "I think we should visit more places like this along the coast."

"Samantha Benson, are you hinting at something?"

"Like what?" I ask, genuinely confused. I take the cone back and take a bite of cream and waffle. So. Freaking. Good.

Jensen shrugs. "We've never really talked about it, about us living together."

My brows pinch together. "We *do* live together."

He holds up a finger as his lips bunch. "Good point."

I moved in with Jensen and his moms six months ago. At first, I thought it would be odd, the four of us living under the same roof. As the days ticked by, though, it was nothing like I expected. Liz and Tiffany respect our space and don't helicopter parent us. Which is nice, considering we are adults.

"What I meant," he says, lowering his hand. "Is us living together on our own. Just me and you."

Oh. *Oh.* Hello, next step. Not that the next step scares me. With Jensen, every step is inevitable.

"That's kind of big for us," I say. His frame wilts and eyes grow sullen. "But I'm ready if you are," I rush to add.

A hint of color returns to his face, along with his bright smile. "Thank God." He lays a hand over his heart. "I was worried for a second."

I lean forward and press a kiss to his lips. "Jensen Page, you never need to worry about us." Then I kiss him again. "Now…" I hold the cone between us. "Help me finish this so we can go to the market for Ma."

"Yes, ma'am, Sam." He smirks, takes the cone and bites a chunk of it off.

If this is day one of our vacation, I can't wait to see what the next six days have in store. Being in this place with Jensen feels magical. Like all our dreams are possible. Him saying he wants us to take the next step… that is definitely a step in the right direction. And I look forward to walking the path with him.

THREE

JENSEN

We walk along the water's edge, hand in hand. Mom and Ma twenty feet ahead of us and Haystack Rock not too far in the distance.

Cannon Beach is so different from Los Angeles. Back home, life is always go, go, go. In this place, life is calm and magical and limitless. A breath of fresh air. Here, anything feels possible. Here, wishes and dreams come true.

Before the end of our trip, I want only one birthday wish to come true.

Months ago, when the moms mentioned this trip, an idea popped into my head. An idea I have yet to speak aloud. Not yet. Not until I summon the nerve. Because this idea of mine… it will change us forever. Hopefully for the better.

I can't put it off much longer. Ready or not, that day is almost here. So close, I all but taste it on my tongue.

"It's so quiet here," Sam says softly, then giggles. "Almost feels like I'll be scolded by the librarian for talking too loud."

Twisting, I kiss her crown and hug her closer to my side. "Right? Such a contrast from home."

She takes a deep breath and tightens her hold on my arm. "Never thought I'd enjoy a place like this. Small towns and quiet beaches." Her head tips back and her unique blue gaze locks with mine. "Now, I have a new outlook."

"Agreed." My mouth drops to hers in a chaste kiss. "I love the city. Love working side by side with Ma in the kitchen. Love the bustle and lights and endless things to do. But this place..." I stare out to sea. Get lost in the tide and the skyline as sunset nears. Then I look back at my girl. "Is it weird that I could see us in a place like this?"

Sam swallows before our eyes disconnect. We meander along the shoreline in comfortable silence. Every now and again, I peek down at her. Watch as her eyes rove the ocean, the mountains, the larger-than-life evergreen trees. Take her in as she studies the landscape so incomparable to the city we have always known.

The moms turn around and lead the way back to the cottage. With each step forward, the sun slowly dips lower in the western sky. Adds yellow and orange and various shades of pink to the darkening blue sky. I breathe in the salty air. Bask in the warmth where Sam's skin connects with mine. Close my eyes for one, two, three steps and stash this moment in my mental scrapbook.

"It isn't weird," Sam whispers, snapping my attention back to her.

I peek down at her as she shrugs and gives a lopsided grin. Loose strands from her ponytail tickle her face as the fading light adds a glow to her skin. In this moment, I can't help but think how damn lucky I am to have this woman in my life. The way we met wasn't ideal. But I thank my lucky stars for every moment—good and bad—that led me to her.

Samantha Benson is my saving grace. My person. Without her, life wouldn't have as much hope or purpose or heart. For as long as she stands beside me, life will always be worth living. For as long as she holds my heart in her hands, I will know love.

"Really?" I bite back a smile. "So if I suggested we move here, you wouldn't freak out?" Even if I wanted to live in a place like Cannon Beach, I would sit down with Sam and discuss it. Hash out the details, the pros and cons.

Structure is a must for us both. Not hardcore, everything-we-do-must-be-planned structure. But day-to-day routines keep us grounded. If either of us wanted to move, we would sit down and sort through every facet with a fine-tooth comb. Where and when. What we would do for work and pleasure when we got there. Why we chose the location. Why we would be happy there. Every attribute involved.

"Uh…" Her eyes widen slightly as she clamps down on her lips. "Maybe a little." She swallows, then relaxes her shoulders an inch. "What would we do here? You work for Ma, and I don't picture them leaving LA anytime soon. Finding a retail job in a new town wouldn't be a challenge for me. Maybe the sweet shop." Mischief glints her eyes on the last part.

Moving isn't at the top of the list, but I love how easily Sam is willing to explore life with me in a new place. If we left Los Angeles, it wouldn't be anytime soon. First, I would want to visit more places. Other small towns. Places bigger than a small town, but smaller than a big city. See which calls to my heart and hers. Then we would talk logistics.

"Just an idea." I wrap both my arms around her middle and kiss her crown as we walk wobbly along the surf. "We haven't seen enough of the world to know where we want to put down roots." I inhale deeply. "But something about this place is —"

"Charming? Incredible? Enchanting?"

I laugh. "All of the above."

We walk up the steep incline from the beach to the cottage. Ma announces dinner will be ready in an hour. Rather than follow her inside, I steer Sam over to the semicircle of Adirondack chairs facing the ocean. A small firepit just feet away. Parking Sam in a chair, I trek to the wood bin near the porch stairs.

"Be right back."

Arms loaded with wood, I grab one of the newspapers in the bin and the pack of fireplace matches. Sam's eyes heat my skin as I stack the wood in the firepit, strategically stuff the newspaper below, and light the match. Once the fire catches, I take the chair beside her and extend my hand. Without hesitation, she laces our fingers.

Sunsets and fires and waves crashing in the distance… there is only one thing that would make this moment more perfect with Sam. One thing I have considered countless times, but haven't followed through with. Yet.

Much as I wish tonight was the night, I know it isn't. But the day is fast approaching.

Days after the moms approached me about a birthday trip to Cannon Beach, I scoured the internet for things to do and places to explore. Recently, Sam and I started hiking more. But we haven't spread our wings much. Haven't traveled too far from the city. I didn't know a lot about Oregon but knew there would be plenty of places for us to explore.

Hours of research and planning led me to the perfect spot. The exact location I want to take Sam. Every picture I saw online has breathtaking views. Hard as it has been, I have kept our upcoming excursion top secret. The moms don't even know what I have up my sleeve. But they will soon enough.

"We should make s'mores one night."

I squeeze Sam's fingers. "We definitely should.

Maybe one of the shops in town has specialty marsh-mallows."

Sam spins to face me, her face aglow from the fire and the idea of homemade flavored marshmallows. "You really do know my heart, Jensen Page."

I lift her hand and bring her knuckles to my lips. "Thank you for letting me know your heart."

Going into town in search of s'mores supplies is the perfect excuse to visit more shops. Although I know Sam better than I know myself, what I have planned needs to go off without hiccups. I need supplies. Items that can be bought under the guise of Ma needing them.

Over the next few days, the goal is to line every-thing up for the big day. A day none of us will forget.

We came to Cannon Beach to celebrate my birth-day. When we leave, we will have something else to celebrate. I hope.

FOUR

SAMANTHA

Something is up with Jensen. Long as we have known each other, I know when things aren't one hundred percent with him. And something is definitely off.

"You feeling alright?" I ask, stepping up behind him and wrapping my arms around his waist. I rest my cheek between his shoulder blades and take a deep breath.

Jensen blankets my arms with his and tightens my hold on him. "Yeah. Of course. Why do you ask?" The words rush from his lips, which only solidifies my concern.

I loosen my grip on him and step around to his front. His smoky-topaz irises lock with my blues and, for a beat, we breathe each other in. Hints of purple highlight the skin beneath his veiny eyes. I lift my hands to cup his cheeks and swipe my thumbs over the evidence of his exhaustion. His eyes drift shut as his shoulders bow.

"What's wrong?"

He leans more into my touch before turning to kiss my palm. "Nothing. Just haven't slept well." His eyes open and roam my face. "Probably the mattress or sleeping in an unfamiliar place." Jensen twirls the end of my hair around his fingers and follows the movement with his eyes. "Promise I'm fine."

Pushing up on my toes, I press my lips to his. The kiss is soft and sweet for one, two, three breaths. Jensen swipes his tongue along the seam of my lips then pushes inside and deepens the kiss. His strong arms band around my waist and lift me off the floor. I wrap my arms around him. Comb my fingers through his long locks. Melt into his frame as he holds me to him.

All too soon, he breaks the kiss. Plants me back on my feet. Cups my cheeks in his hands and holds my gaze.

I push out my bottom lip and he chuckles. "What if I wasn't done kissing you?"

He drops a peck on my lips. "More kisses later. Promise." Another kiss on the tip of my nose. "You get ready while I scope out the kitchen for hiking snacks."

I narrow my eyes at him. Scan his eyes and lips for a tell—any tell—that will express what he isn't saying. He says it's the mattress or possibly being in a new place that has him not sleeping. But I *know* Jensen.

Which means I know something else is eating away at him.

Jensen and I may not know the entire kitchen inventory, but we have a rough idea of what snacks are available. Heck, we tossed half the items in the cart. So why does he need to go check them? Not like the moms would eat all our excursion snacks.

Weird. He is acting super weird.

Exhaustion does strange things to people, but I have never seen Jensen so… antsy and drained.

"Maybe we should just stay in today. I'll catch up on my book while you nap."

"No," he says with a shake of his head. "Swear, I'm all good." He chuckles. "I'll have Ma make me one of those super green smoothies that I hate but she swears by."

Stepping into him once more, I cup his cheek. "Fine," I huff out. "Just don't want you passing out on the trail. At least tell the moms where we'll be, in case reception sucks."

Our hiking trip today… it is a big fat secret. Jensen refuses to spill the beans. To any of us. But if he is dead on his feet, someone needs to know where we will be. I don't foresee us getting lost or getting in a showdown with a bear, but you never know.

He kisses the heart of my palm. "I'll tell them while I'm in the kitchen. Now go." He shoos me away. "Get ready. I'll be back in a sec."

As I head for the bathroom, Jensen exits the room.

Under the warm spray of the shower, my mind runs rampant. Returns to the days of Lewis House and shortly thereafter. The stress and heartache and life-altering revelations that came about.

Please let exhaustion be the only thing weighing him down.

With our messy pasts, it isn't difficult for either of us to shove hurt, tension, or burdens aside. To mask them with big smiles and words of reassurance. To put on a show while our demons eat us alive.

During the hike, I will store my worry in the *deal with it later* pile. But the moment we return home, if I don't see his smile, his real smile, I refuse to let it go. Refuse to drop the subject until he tells me what has him restless.

I love Jensen too much. And he would do the same for me in a heartbeat.

FIVE

JENSEN

Yep, I am going to puke.

Why did I tell myself this was a good idea? Not the three-mile trail—I have barely broken a sweat during the hike. But bringing Sam out here, to this epic place, with the intent of getting down on one knee and proposing.

Because you love her, dumbass.

Because I love her and can't imagine a single day of the future without her.

One after another, I take deep breaths as we approach the lookout. During my hours of online research before the trip, one spot kept popping up in my search of Cannon Beach hiking trails. An elevated view of Cannon Beach from the trail in Ecola State Park. The spot had been marked by countless hikers on a trails app. A spot we are now mere feet from.

Please, God, don't let me puke. Not now.

Sam peels her pack from her shoulders and sets it on the ground. She steps close to the edge of the view point, props her hands on her hips, and inhales deeply as she takes in the view.

"Wow," she says, barely above a whisper.

Wow is my exact thought as I take in the sight of her in this place. Her dark locks, secured in a ponytail, fly with the breeze. Her profile brighter with the smile on her lips. And the way her whole body comes alive at the view… it steals my breath.

Damn, I am a lucky man.

Unshouldering my own pack, I set it beside hers. But I don't step up next to her to look at the sights. There will be time for that later.

Instead, I dig inside my right front pocket and pull out the rose gold band with a much larger opal than her promise ring. A ring that signifies much more than the promise of *one day.* This ring is a vow of forever. Something I can't wait to start with Sam.

Two more deep breaths—in and out, in and out. I inch closer to where she stands but stay back and just out of her line of sight. Then I drop on one knee, ignore the bite of rocks in my flesh, and hold the ring up as I wait for Sam to turn around and spot me.

"Jensen, what're you—" Sam spins around in search of me and slaps a hand over her mouth. "Oh my…" Tears well in her eyes as she stumbles closer.

"Jensen." My name is a whisper on her lips. "Oh my god."

Sweat slicks my skin as my heart races. A fresh bout of nausea hits. And I can't seem to catch my breath.

"Sam," I croak out, then clear my throat. "Sam, I had this whole day mapped out. Wanted to make it as special for you as you are to me. I never thought I'd be this nervous. That I'd lose sleep and be so beside myself." I laugh and Sam joins in. "I loved you before I put a promise ring on your finger. Before we decided to be more than friends. But I didn't want to rush you or us. You mean the world to me, Samantha Benson." I take a deep breath and swallow the emotional lump in my throat. "And I'd love nothing more than if you'd be my wife. If you'd stand by me forever."

Tears trail parallel lines on her cheeks, but she doesn't move or wipe them away. She simply stares at me, full of shock and awe.

"Sam, will you marry me?"

My heart bangs wildly against my rib cage as I wait for Sam to react. As I wait for her to answer. Say yes and wrap her arms around my neck. Say yes and beg me to slip the ring on her finger. Say yes and announce our engagement to the world from the cliffside.

But she hasn't moved. Hasn't said a word.

Has she taken a breath in the last minute?

Shit.

Did I get this all wrong? Did I misinterpret the signs? Does she not want to marry me?

Bile claws up my throat and hits the back of my mouth. Dread floods my bloodstream and situates itself in every cell in my body. With each new breath, my body sags forward another inch. Caves in on itself. Starts the process of shutting down, of going into protection mode.

If this is it, if this is the end of us, I won't survive. Sam is my lifeline. The one person I lean on when life gets too heavy. My North Star in the darkest nights. The shining beacon of hope in my life.

She can't say no. She can't.

Off in the distance, I hear my name. Soft like the wind. Floating in on a wispy cloud. Then I hear it again, this time louder, as my body shudders.

"Jensen! Jensen!" I blink a few times. Work to focus my vision, to come out of the dark fog. Notice Sam has her hands on my shoulders and shakes them with a firm grip. "Can you hear me, Jensen?"

My eyes lift to hers and I blink again, watching as she comes into focus. "Sorry."

Sam drops to her knees in front of me and frames my face in her palms. "You scared me half to death."

My brows tighten at the middle. "What?"

She drops her forehead to mine. Her breath hot and ragged on my lips. Nose grazing the side of mine. "I wiped the tears from my eyes, ready to say yes, and saw you pale as a ghost." Sam strengthens her hold on my cheeks. "Don't do that to me again." Her words are hoarse and jagged and panicky.

Damn, I didn't mean to frighten her.

Out of everything to leave her lips, all I hear is that she said yes. *Yes!* Sam said yes. She wants to marry me. Wants to be mine forever. Wants to share a life together until we are old and gray and crotchety.

She said yes! Sam said yes!

I drop my lips to hers and kiss her as if it is our last. Kiss her with every ounce of love and passion I hold in my heart for her.

"Didn't mean to frighten you," I say as I break the kiss. "Sorry." Then my lips drop back to hers. I relish in the taste of her. Allow her warmth to bring me back to life. Bask in the reality of what just happened. Sooner than desirable, I break the kiss and drop my forehead to hers. "Did you say yes? You'll marry me?"

She leans back, combs her fingers through my hair, and follows the action with her eyes. She takes a deep breath as her eyes find mine once more. Her beautiful smile slowly plumps her cheeks. "You make me laugh."

I tilt my head to the side, curious what she means. By no means am I a comedian, but I have my moments. "Oh, yeah?"

She nods. "Yep. You ask if I'll marry you as if there was another option."

I open my mouth to say she always has a choice, but she cuts me off with a finger pressed to my lips.

"It has never been a matter of *will* I marry you. It's always been a matter of *when*."

No use in fighting the cheek-stinging smile on my face.

"Jensen, it has always been you."

I speak up before she stops me again. "Always been you too, Sam." Tucking a few flyaway strands of hair behind her ear, I press a chaste kiss to her lips. "God, I love you."

"And I love you." She swipes her thumbs across my cheeks and sighs. "Now…" I meet her expectant gaze as she drops her left hand from my cheek and holds it out between us. "I believe you have something for me."

Laughter threatens to spill from my lips, but I bite it back. We have a lifetime to laugh together. Right now, I want to slip forever onto her left ring finger and share with the world that Samantha Benson will soon be my wife. The woman I will confide in and love and cherish as long as there is breath in my lungs and blood in my veins.

"Thank you for loving me, Sam," I say as I slide the ring in place.

I loved her radiant smile before, but the one lighting her face right now… I want this smile every day of forever. Will do whatever it takes to see it daily. Because our love makes her glow.

Luckiest. Man. Alive.

"Thank you for letting me love you."

"Now, let's go tell the world."

Right there, on the edge of a cliff in Cannon Beach, Oregon, we shout from the top of our lungs.

"Samantha Benson said yes!"

"Jensen Page is my forever!"

Then we hike the rest of the trail, hand in hand, as if today is the start of our forever. Without a doubt, it definitely is. Because wherever Sam is, that is my forever.

October—one year later

WHEN JENSEN ASKED ME TO MARRY HIM LAST YEAR, I knew it wouldn't be long before I took the last name Page. We had known each other for years. Our love brewed slow and over time. Lingered in the background as we connected on a friendship level. Blossomed after the first time he took my hand and I knew he was *more*. Flourished as we spent more time with each other and linked our lives in new ways.

When Jensen proposed, it hadn't been too soon. Deep in my bones, I have always been certain this day would come. Us picking a date one year later hadn't been soon enough. Although eager to say *I do*, we both wanted the day to be perfect. So we opted to not rush down the aisle.

I never pictured myself in lace or tulle or princess-type dresses. No one will ever describe me as either girly or tomboy. Unintentionally, I land somewhere in the middle. Dresses and hoodies, soft colors and dark, my closet is full of it all. My attire varies with my moods. I wear what catches my eye and feels good on my skin. I don't care for labels and wear what makes *me* happy.

So when the moms sat down with me and asked if I wanted a wedding organizer for the big day, I shrugged. Didn't I just need to buy a dress, find a notary, and ask the small circle of loved ones to be present? Why on earth would I need an organizer for that?

Like a person with no clue, I'd told them yes.

In no time, the simple, small affair I pictured in my head turned into something much more. A grand soiree. Ma is catering the day, of course. But now there is a florist, deejay, bartender, and venue.

"This is a big day, sweetheart. A day it's okay to go all out." Mom's words from almost a year ago repeat in my head. *"Big days should be celebrated like no other. One day, you'll look back at the photos and appreciate all the special touches."*

Although I didn't want a grandiose event, she was right. The closer it got to our wedding day, the more I appreciated the finer details. Flowers and centerpieces and guest gifts that were neutral with a rustic feminine touch. Ma decorated the cake to match the decor. When she mentioned a naked cake with sage leaves and baby roses to match my bouquet, I furrowed my brow. Wasn't until I saw an example that it clicked in place.

"Need help?" Mom asks as I unzip the bag holding my dress.

"Please."

Once we have the dress out, I step into the chiffon skirt and hold the lace halter over my bust. Mom darts to my back side and fastens the buttons at my lower back before the one at the back of my neck. Never in my life have I felt like a princess. Until this moment.

I face the full-length mirror and study my own reflection. Not that I have never worn a dress, but this… no dress will compare. *My wedding dress.*

"Beautiful," Mom whispers. "Jensen will lose his mind when he sees you."

"In a good way, I hope."

A soft smile lights her face. "In the best way."

Mom helps me add the final touch with a pair of pearl strand earrings. Simple and classic, yet they bring the whole ensemble together. As she fetches my bouquet, music starts outside. A cue that I have a minute or two left.

"You've always held a special place in my heart, Samantha." Mom hands me the bouquet and offers her arm. "I am so grateful Jensen has you in his life. The love you two share is like nothing I've known."

I tip my face to the sky and blink.

"And I can't wait to be your actual mom. Well, mother-in-law. Not that titles matter with us."

"Glad I don't wear much makeup," I say with a laugh.

"Sorry to make you cry, sweetheart." She plucks a tissue from the box nearby and blots under my eyes. "Better grab more. We'll need them."

A knock sounds on the door and we both startle. Mom cracks the door open and chats with whoever is on the other side. Before I catch anything, the door closes and Mom faces me with a glowing smile.

"It's time."

She offers her arm once more and I hook mine with hers. I take a deep breath as she opens the door and we walk toward my future. Toward Jensen.

JENSEN

The music changes and signals Sam's entrance at any moment. I tighten and relax my fingers. Park my hands in front of my waist, then move them back to my sides.

No one told me where to put my hands.

When we took my annual birthday trip last year, I planned to propose to my best friend and love of my life. I scoured the internet for days in search of the perfect spot to ask Sam to be my wife. Minus my momentary freak-out, the proposal went off without a hitch.

After we left Cannon Beach, I hoped one day to return. Not only is the town fun and eclectic and pleas-ant, it now holds wonderful memories. Memories I will never forget.

Today, Sam and I are adding to those memories.

As we sat down to plan our wedding, I hadn't expected for it to be in the same town where I proposed. When Sam suggested the idea, I'd answered with a resounding yes. From that point forward, everything flowed seamlessly as we planned our big day. And with luck on our side, we were also able to reserve the same cottage.

Sam rounds the corner of the house along the patio, her elbow hooked on Mom's arm. And damn... she steals the breath from my lungs. Tears sting the backs of my eyes as I take her in.

My wife. My forever.

The halter bust of her dress is woven lace while the floor-length skirt floats over the earth and behind her. Her dark locks are secured in a low, messy bun above the nape of her neck while a few straggler strands wisp over her cheeks. Makeup soft and neutral and just enough to highlight her already beautiful features.

Without effort, she stuns me with her ethereal appearance. My heart beats, beats, beats against my sternum as I memorize this moment. Take mental photographs of this gorgeous woman. A woman that will be by my side forever.

Three more steps and Sam stands across from me at the altar. Mom unhooks her elbow from Sam then takes her seat in the front row next to Ma. After a deep inhale, I lock eyes with Sam and everyone else disappears. In this moment, it is only me and her and the minister—but I tune his words out too.

"I love you," I mouth to Sam.

"Love you too."

The next blip of time is a blur. Sam and I speak when we are supposed to, say our I dos, and add the most precious pieces of jewelry to our fingers. Cheers erupt around us as the minister pronounces us husband and wife. A few snarky comments hit the air when I kiss Sam like no one is here—not that I care. She's *my* wife and I will kiss her how I want to.

As the wedding ends and the reception begins, we all let go. Party like we always would and not in a stuffy formal way. The only difference is the awesome food spread and an incredible cake.

Congratulations are shared and a mountain of gifts are opened from family and friends. Aunt Sarah, Uncle Jackson, and my two little cousins, Alexandria and Anderson. Aunt Christy, Uncle Rick, Aunt Ella, and Uncle Thomas. Grandma and Grandpa Warren as well as Grandma and Grandpa Page. Ms. Lewis and Dr. Long from Lewis House.

So much love in one place. Love I am eternally grateful to have from each of them. Without them, who knows where Sam and I would be today. If we would be who we are today. Safe and happy and loved. And with each other.

"Time for cake," Ma announces.

Sam and I shuffle to the end of the kitchen counter.

I pick up the cake knife and Sam places her hand over mine. Cameras flash throughout the room as we cut the cake and hold a slice to feed one another.

"I love you," she says, "but if you smash cake in my face, I may get violent."

I snicker. "Is that so?" She doesn't say a word as she nods. I hold up my slice. "Here's to the sweetest forever." I bring the cake to her lips. Just as she opens her mouth, I smash the cake against her lips and cheek.

Three methodical breaths pass as Sam remains perfectly still. I stare at her, a ticking time bomb waiting to detonate. A wicked grin curls the corners of her mouth. A grin that should scare me, but doesn't. If anything, it eggs me on.

"Sweetest forever, huh?" she asks and I nod slowly.

She brings the slice of cake to my lips and I brace for the onslaught. But it doesn't come. She simply lets me bite the cake. The crowd *awes* at the display and I face them with a smile.

Bad move.

The second I look away from Sam, cake gets smeared into my hair and down my jaw and neck. Laughter floods the room just as another piece hits me, again and again.

I manage to get my arms around Sam and pin hers down. "Okay, okay." I laugh. "Sorry." My lips press to hers. "Please, stop. Let everyone else have cake too." Another kiss. "I deserved all the cake to the face."

"Yes, you did."

"But now…"

Sam lifts her chin and looks me square in the eye. "Now…"

"Now, I just want you. My Sam. Sweeter than any confection."

She plants a kiss on my lips. "Love you, Jensen."

"Love you more, Sam."

***

Did you first meet Jensen and Samantha in Beloved Devotion, Liz and Tiffany's story? When I wrote Beloved Devotion, I always wanted more of Jensen and Sam. Wanted to see them find their HEA. And I'm so pleased I got to write this short story for them.

Distorted Devotion

Swept off her feet by love, life takes a dark, unexpected turn. Now the love of her life may be the cause of her death. Check out this gripping, romantic suspense.

Undying Devotion

A long-term couple with a secret life. Their friends envy the bond they share, but remain oblivious to their lifestyle and how deep the bond lies. A turn of events has her wanting to spill every secret.

Beloved Devotion

She asks the love of her life to marry her. When her girlfriend hesitates, then says yes, she is determined to learn why. As the pieces start to fall in place, she discovers she doesn't know her fiancée at all.

The Click Duet

High school sweethearts torn apart. When fate gives them a second chance, one doesn't trust they won't be hurt again. Through the Lens (Click Duet #1) and Time Exposure (Click Duet #2) is an angsty, second chance, friends to lovers romance with all the feels.

The Inked Duet

A man with a broken heart and a woman scared to put herself out there. Love is never easy. Sometimes love rips you apart. Fine Line (Inked Duet #1) and Love Buzz (Inked Duet #2) is a second chance at love, single parent romance with a pinch of angst and dash of suspense.

The Insomniac Duet

He was her high school bully. She was the outcast that secretly crushed on him. More than ten years later, he's her boss, completely oblivious to their shared past, and wants no one but her. More importantly, he doesn't understand her animosity toward him.

Transcendental

A musician in search of his muse and a woman grieving the loss of her husband. Two weeks at an exclusive retreat and their connection rivals all others. Until she leaves early without notice. But he refuses to give up until he finds her again.

Depths Awakened

A small town romance which captivates you from the start. Two broken souls have sworn off love. Vowed to never lose anyone else. But their undeniable attraction brings them together and refuses to let go.

Connect with Persephone

www.persephoneautumn.com

Subscribe to Persephone's Newsletter

www.persephoneautumn.com/newsletter

Join Persephone's Reader Group

Persephone's Playground

Follow Persephone Online

instagram.com/persephoneautumn

facebook.com/persephoneautumnwrites

tiktok.com/@persephoneautumn

goodreads.com/persephoneautumn

bookbub.com/authors/persephone-autumn

amazon.com/author/persephoneautumn

pinterest.com/persephoneautumn

twitter.com/PersephoneAutum

ACKNOWLEDGMENTS

When it comes time to write acknowledgments, sometimes I wonder if I express myself enough. There are so many to be thankful when it comes to putting a book in the world.

To my family and close friends… thank you for always supporting my need to write. Whether it sweet, hot and steamy, dark, or absolutely bizarre, you are my biggest cheerleaders. I love you all so much and wouldn't have made it this far without any of you!

To Ellie and Rosa… you ladies are in my top 5! Thank you for always making my manuscripts better, questioning what the hell I mean sometimes, and giving me the best feedback always. Can't wait to hug you soon!

To Abi… thank you for giving Sweetest Devotion a beautiful new cover! You gave this entire series new life and I'm eternally grateful!

To my readers… yes, you! Thank you for picking up my books and reading my words. Every time someone says they've read a book of mine, I cry—internally and externally. Your love for my stories keeps me going. For that, I send a million hugs to you!

ABOUT THE AUTHOR

Persephone Autumn lives in Florida with her wife, crazy dog, and two lover-boy cats. A proud mom with a cuckoo grandpup. An ethnic food enthusiast who has fun discovering ways to veganize her favorite non-vegan foods. If given the opportunity, she would intentionally get lost in nature.

For years, Persephone did some form of writing; mostly journaling or poetry. After pairing her poetry with images and posting them online, she began the journey of writing her first novel.

She mainly writes romance and poetry, but on occasion dips her toes in other works. Look for her non-romance publications under P. Autumn.